If Pigs Wore Wigs

BY JERYL CHRISTMAS

This Book Belongs To

_____

LET

GO ...

AND JUST IMAGINE ...

IF pigs wore wigs,
then a horse, of course,
would want to wear one too.

These three would be
the rage on stage
from here to Timbuktu.

AND ...

IF llamas wore pajamas,
a giraffe would laugh
to see this delightful crew.

"Hee Hee!"

A crocodile's smile

and the grin on a hen

would show their amusement too.

OR ...

IF a hawk had a talk
with her chick who was sick
'cause he'd eaten every worm ...

a wren would lend

some nice advice

on manners he should learn.

THEN ...

IF a crab in a cab
saw a toad by the road
and decided to give him a ride ...

a frog on a log

and a bear in a chair

would sneak in the other side.

ALSO ...

IF a goat in a boat
pulled a float by a rope,
what fun there would be on the lake!

Bees on skis
and a deer on the pier
would enjoy their afternoon break.

AND ...

IF a shark shot a dart
at the tail of a whale
and started to cause a revolt ...

there's a cure for sure
from the feel of an eel
with a sizzling electric jolt!

THEN ...

IF a shrimp had a limp
or a clam had a jam,
and he couldn't open his shell ...

the croc who's a doc

and his nurse with a purse

would come to make them well.

BUT ...

IF a squid always did
what the fish only wish
that they were able to do ...

the sea would be
all ink and stink
and turn all shades of blue.

AND ...

IF a fox opened locks
for an ape to escape,
it would cause quite a hectic scene ...

if the goose got loose
and the yaks left tracks
and made a mess to clean.

NEXT ...

IF a cow pushed a plow
and a crow had a hoe,
this farmer would be aghast ...

but if a snake swung a rake
while a snail held the pail,
he'd take off **very** fast!

FINALLY ...

"HELP!"

IF all came together
like birds of a feather
and joined in a huge group hug ...

a porcupine
wouldn't even mind
a hug from a slimy slug.

EWWW!

The End

www.ingramcontent.com/pod-product-compliance
Lightning Source LLC
Chambersburg PA
CBHW041007170626
46815CB00002B/203